"Now, listen, Eugene, my grandma is nice. But she pinches my cheeks a lot and her house is full of funny old stuff. She's always cooking and she talks funny, too. And, Eugene, . . .

WATCH OUT FOR THE CHICKEN FEET IN YOUR SOUP

story and pictures by Tomie de Paola

Aladdin Paperbacks

FOR AUNTS KATE, CLOTILDA + CLORINDA ♡ ♡ ♡

Aladdin Paperbacks
An imprint of Simon & Schuster
Children's Publishing Division
1230 Avenue of the Americas
New York, NY 10020
Copyright © 1974 by Tomie dePaola
All rights reserved including the right of reproduction
in whole or in part in any form.
Printed in the United States of America
20   19   18   17   16
Library of Congress Cataloging in Publication Data
dePaola, Thomas Anthony
Watch out for the chicken feet in your soup.
SUMMARY: Embarrassed to introduce a friend to his
old-fashioned Italian grandmother, a young boy
gains a new appreciation of her when he finds
how well she and his friend get along.
[1. Grandparents—Fiction]   I. Title.
PZ7.D439Wat   [E]   74-8201

ISBN 0-671-66745-9

"Joey, mio bambino!
How nice you come to
see grandma."

"Grandma,
this is my friend,
Eugene."

"That's nice. You bring
Eugeney to see grandma.
Come in, ragazzi."

"It's Eugene, ma'am."

"What's your grandma doing with our coats?"

"How nice you bring your nice coats to keep grandma's bread dough warm, so it rise nice."

"Caro come!
You, my Joey and Eugeney,
I give you something nice to eat.
Zuppa, nice chicken soup."

"It's Eugene, ma'am."

"Psst, Joey, look!"

"Just for you nice boys . . . spaghetti. Mangia!"

"Ugh! I'm full!"

"I love spaghetti!"

"Joey! You not eating! Eugeney eat every-thing all up. You not going to grow up big and strong like Eugeney. Eugeney, you come with Joey's grandma and help her make her nice bread!"

"We push the dough."

"Now we braid the dough and make circles and dolls."

"I'm finished!"

"Now we put it all in the oven and bake it nice and brown."

"Joey, you take this home to your mama."

"And this is for my Joey!

Because you my special Joey."

"Arrivederci, Joey, Eugeney."

BREAD DOLLS

Tomie de Paola had an old-fashioned grandmother just like **Joey's.** "She was wonderful to me," he says. "And her **bread dolls were a** special treat. I'll never forget its delicious smell as it was baking in the oven. She never shared her recipes, but after years of experimenting this is how I figure she made those wonderful dolls."

Scald **¼ cup of milk.** Add **½ cup shortening.** While this is cooling, mix **4 cups of sifted flour, ¾ cup sugar, 1 tsp. salt and 1 tsp. cinnamon** in a large bowl. Set aside.

Dissolve **1 package of dry yeast** into **⅛ cup warm water.** Sprinkle **½ tsp. sugar** on top to activate yeast.

Make a well in flour mixture. Beat slightly **4 eggs** and pour into the well along with shortening and yeast mixtures. Mix together thoroughly.

Turn out on floured board and knead until smooth and elastic. Put the dough back in bowl and brush top with oil. Then cover with wax paper and a towel and set in a warm place until it doubles in bulk. This should take about 2 hours. Punch it back down and knead slightly. Let it set for 5 minutes and heat the oven at 350°.

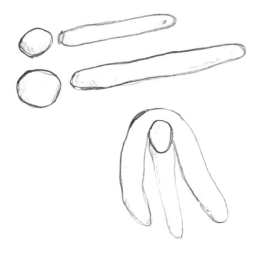

On a cookie sheet divide the dough into 3 lemon-sized pieces and 3 orange-sized pieces. Roll the pieces into ropes. Place an **uncooked egg** on end of short rope.

Place long rope around egg. Braid. Cover with dish towels and let rise again. Mix an egg yolk with a bit of water and brush over doll. Bake about 45 minutes.